Sharanagati
Born for Adventure

Govinda Goshala
Cow Haven

LINDA VOITH

and Bhargav Talajia

Govinda Goshala
Cow Haven

Dear reader: If you enjoy this book, please share with your friends, place it in your local library, or help a goshala near you. By getting involved, you can ensure a future in which more cows will be able to live their lives in a loving and safe home.

Print version for Amazon Digital Platafform.

Sharanagati Born for Adventure

This is a book about a calf named Sharanagati. (Shah-rah-nah-gah-tee)

You can call her Shara if you like.

Tips for reading the book

Read the main story line on each page first. Then go back and see what butterfly and bee have to tell Sharanagati. Then watch the videos.

Buzy Bee and Butterfly have weaved in two science based tool to help kids stay calm when they are having a hard time. Parents can benefit from them too. Make a game of it and see if you, and your kids, can coach each other, (and Sharanagati), to use them.

1) Taking a full breath in, followed by a long slow breath out, is known to calm the nervous system. The full breath re-inflates the lungs. The emphasis on the gentle slow exhale, releases carbon dioxide and brings calm to body and mind.

2) Looking at something far away in the distance, or at a horizon, is also know to calm the nervous system.

Sharanagati, always listen to your heart. Your adventures will start soon.

There is a reason you were born with a lightning stripe!

Hi my name is Sharanagati. When I was born, I felt as though I was ready for adventure. But I lived at a dairy farm, inside a small pen. How could I get out and have fun?

What's a Goshala?

It's a sanctuary for cows

One day, two friendly people came to visit. They were looking for a calf to take home to their Go-sha-lah.

Steve and Linda said I could come home to live with them, and their animal friends. I was so excited.

 That's so mean!

That's just the way that goats play with each other.

As soon as I walked into the barn, I saw the goats. They were shocked to see a baby cow. They were nervous and challenged me to fight.

I did NOT want to fight. But I did have a lot of fun running around the barn, playing tag with the goats.

 Oh! they are getting to know each other

Cows love their babies

There was a cow at the goshala whose name was Shanti. She was my grandma. We were so happy to meet each other.

I had a wonderful time drinking milk from Shanti. Her milk was warm and delicious. I felt safe and happy when I drank her milk.

There were lots of people who came to help out at the Goshala.
Soon I had many friends. I never felt lonely.

She is always hungry.

That's because she is growing so fast!

During the day, my Grandma Shanti would go to graze in the big pasture with the other cows. When I got hungry, my friends fed me a bottle for a snack.

I loved my new home. I got to run around outside all day.

Remember, everything you see is part of God's creation.

He is near and far. He is in your heart, looking out for you.

When I got bored, Steve took me for walks around the the neighborhood. Sometimes I got scared by things I had never seen before. We practiced looking far away at the horizon. It helped me feel calm.

I hope she doesn't lose the butterfly
marking on her forehead. It's so cute.

As I grew bigger, my coat started to change colors from brown to black. I was worried that the white lightning stripe on my shoulder would fade away.

You will always keep your special markings, Sharanagati. They are blessings.

My lightning stripe reminded me to be adventurous.

The bigger I got, the more I loved eating grass. I would eat and eat until my belly was full. Then I would go inside the barn to take a nap. But one day, I ate so much, that I could not squeeze through the door. I was stuck on the outside of the barn.

Sharanagati, You can sleep with us under the stars.

Camping is fun.

Next time you get worried take a deep breath in, and a long slow breath out.

It will help you calm down.

Linda saw that I was stranded outside. She ran to get a saw and a hammer. Linda cut some boards off the barn. She made the door bigger so that I could get back inside.

That night, my Grandma did not come back to the barn with the other cows. I missed Grandma Shanti! Linda went to look for her in the pasture. Grandma had just given birth to a new baby.

I was so happy when Grandma Shanti came back to the barn! What a surprise it was to see my new little sister. I wanted to play, but Krishi was too wobbly.

Grandma Shanti said she still loved me. Now she needed my help to take care of the new baby. Krishi was very little and needed extra attention.

Krishi drank a lot of milk every day. Grandma Shanti said that she wanted Krishi to grow up to be big and strong, just like me.

I felt confused when I watched Krishi drinking milk. I liked being a big girl. But I also missed nursing from my grama and getting all the attention.

Even though Grandma Shanti spent a lot of time with both of us. I was still feeling left out.

 Try something new.

It's time for another adventure, Sharanagati

Sometimes I would sneak up behind grandma Shanti and drink a little bit of her milk. I tried to be a baby again. But it just wasn't the same.

 Shyama was afraid of hurting Sharanagati with his big horns.

She was disappointed. He would not wrestle.

I was getting more and more confused and grumpy. I didn't know what to do with all of my energy. I decided to do the most adventurous thing I could think of. I challenged Shyama, the biggest ox at the Goshala to a wrestling match.

I wonder who will win?

They both win, as long as they are both having fun.

Next I decided to wrestle with Chintamani, (chin-tom-ah-knee), the oldest cow at the Goshala. It was fun to wrestle with Chintamani. She was lively, and gentle. She knew how to make playing fun because she had raised five of her own babies.

Chintamani missed having little calves around her. She liked it when I snuggled next to her.

Chintamani spent a lot of time every day giving me baths and playing with me.

Now I have learned to trust the little voice in my heart that encourages me and helps me find ways to have fun wherever I am. That's a good feeling.

I am a lucky cow to have so many human and animal friends who love me. Now that I am all grown up, my favorite adventure is to get petted and brushed by my human friends.

If you would like to get involved and help cows like me and my family to have a safe home, please visit: *Govindagoshala.org* to learn how you can help.

Made in the USA
Middletown, DE
26 April 2022